Carrying a Tree
on the Bus
to Low Edges

Carrying a Tree
on the Bus
to Low Edges

Stephen Sawyer

Smokestack Books
School Farm
Nether Silton
Thirsk
North Yorkshire
YO7 2JZ
e-mail: info@smokestack-books.co.uk
www.smokestack-books.co.uk

ISBN 9781739473488

Smokestack Books
is represented by
Inpress Ltd

for Dad, Mum
and Brother Phillip

Contents

Makes it Rain

I can't see myself for candlelight purling
in metal cups. Goodbyes on the subway wall –
Love Ya Man.   Good guy gone too soon.
A page from *The Star*, his laughter's smile,
I pass him most days, don't know his name.
See you in the next one, Matey.
I can't see myself for a forehead of clear salt,
a chigger of blood in the white of an eye,
the testicles and womb of the sun
drinking potato and tulip wine, taking stock of
passers-by hurrying out of themselves
for staircase light, New York Noir, Cashpoint,
Vamp Store, money homeopathy.
His eyes are silos of pain; his belly is a country
with a hollow skull. If he were a tree
he'd be a tree of black smoke cut down.
If he were a horse he'd wear suspenders
and a powdered wig. *I didn't know you well,*
but you seemed a great kid. I can't see myself
for eyebrows of seaweed, basalt cheekbones
that become lightning anger, nostril violence,
cough and lung spit, centuries of frozen fingers.
Everything always, and never, the same,
broken ranting on the subway stairs ...
I *want Irene...* I *want Irene.* I can't see myself
for death climbing my window in string vest
and y-fronts... *I want Irene... I want Irene...*
his darkened bare footprints lamp cast in snow.
His name is Precipitation. His name is Heaven's
Dark Moan; his heartbeat, a football bouncing
off thigh, instep, window, in childhood waters.
Not many friends out here, you were
one of the few. I can't see myself for distances

undone, the walk of danger balancing the weight
of water on the head, inseparable from a forest
of burning peacocks, a myriad of reflecting eyes
between blazes of sap: saints, martyrs, beggars,
Krishna; a brand tag on a plastic carrier bag
swung into the underpass, the sudden impulse
to beg as a woman from Human Resources
who can't find a parking space,
enters the underworld's anarchy of otherness,
senses the ghost's fear of ghosts as if space
is not made of us. *Should I be walking through*
this man's home? His name is Deluge,
his laughter is a broken rib. If he were a bear,
he'd be named after the First Nation, air-lifted
to an estuary of salmon rivers and sage grass.
If he were a black swan, he'd be a dog bone.
In his dreams of misadventure I appear
with an overzealous usherette as a faucet leak
drips through the ceiling of Film House Four.
He is carried downstream past statues
carved by the virus, barnacled anchors, a lone
leopard seal pup, beheaded forests,
to rock up in the subway like a prophet's eye
before the double take: look away
of people-flowers: purple headed rhododendrons
from the bus depot, a poppy wearing shorts
in the middle of Storm Denis, orchids en route
to the Art School, trumpets on cellular phones
become Winston Wolf. *Can't even say goodbye*
without the council painting over. He dies,
returns unnoticed, already a woman is begging
in his place. I can't see beyond my face
in her face, her face in his face, beyond
wrinkles without a face. She is alone
and not alone, ignored and listened to
by the ignored. Her name is your name,
my name, unnamed; her name is Breaking Water.

You can still be greeted by her hand of smoke.
There she is and isn't in catacombs of cardboard
and sky-less concrete I'd fill in with words
that hear her fingers rolling last year's leaves.
I can't see myself because I am and am not him.
She makes him an oak tree: he enters her shadow.
She is the child who hands you a cloud
that becomes a river. He is the source and mouth
of my blood's ink, the well in the sky
that anoints her forehead, writes me
in sleep. What is the world made of?
She asks a passing prophet wearing glasses.
Makes it rain.

Narcissus' Graves Park Song

Care mongering alchemizes fear into action:
at eight the nationwide clap for key workers.
That first Thursday on opening the door
I thought they were all clapping at me.

'Still at it,' I say on the 'permitted' walk,
'Still at it,' says a familiar face, omitting the 'Yes,'
our three-legged dance as we pass one another,
tall beech and chestnut tenting the winding trail.

Lemon cake in the Rose Garden brings to mind
Proust's madeleines dunked in tea, his fragile
enduring memory. A bristling border terrier takes my
fingers between his teeth, leaving my skin intact.

'You have a friend.' I feel like a twist 'n' treat.
Bilingual branches overhear their own syllabic echo
reveal their pale under tongues, green that is
and isn't green, putting the law of identity

through hoops. Loose bark on a fallen trunk is
a hooded croc's open mouth. We're still using words,
'It's no use to him now, least not as a leg,' says
a woman in bullhorn red tights pushing out

a plastic weight, drawing it in at shoulder height,
'Does he instigate? It doesn't matter.' A half-naked
kite-flyer on his knees praying for a thermal
in the centre circle. What remains of the world?

Seven mongrels, three people and a reek of dung
where five paths meet at Vultures' Banquet.
I am grateful for words that reintroduce the dead,
ventriloquize the living; my great Grandad Ball's

– stretchered off the Somme – in the voice
of my dad: *They'd vote for Adolf Hitler before
Jesus Christ for a penny off the rate of tax.*
What a shock this late on to see truth dance

on a blood-stained stone. The rise in the rate
of death is falling. I am at the bull's eye
of the spherical hour. Lottie, the Shire mare in foal
curves her velvet neck to nip the stock girl
on her shoulder, draws a verbal warning, laughter.

A jet-wing absent blue sky could advertise
ubiquitous water towers, an oak tree speaks to me:
denies it. Evergrey balconies of looping dream:
Joyce Grenfell offers me a custard cream

in the staff common room of *The Happiest Days
of Your Life.* I'll be the film of your body if you'll
be the film of mine. How many poems in a poem?
How many trees in an axe-less world? I see myself

seeing myself in barefooted light, unchained water
fever quick, more real than the body I inhabit.
The stream stammers, argues branch, rock and dog.
I dip into skyward sap write across impurities of air,

every raven in the book of grass 1.5 meters apart.

Ode to the Paint Brush

Paintbrush,
I stare at words
maintain the water level
in your pot, anoint you
with turpentine,
embrace you
with your lathe-turned
shoulders of symmetry.
Forget you. When
did I cross into the room
of sentences?
Your fine filaments
of hog's hair
keep the edge wet,
my words say
what they don't say.
We go on facing
the wooden
trimmings of the world
that remain, unfolding
high gloss reflections
on window sills,
panelled doors. That boy

lifting you from water,
wearing a Stetson,
shooting a cap-gun. Marilyn
singing Happy Birthday
from the crossroads
of her thighs, Kennedy's smile
hazarding retinal damage,
B52s over Vietnam. Paint brush,
I hear your measured breathing

break into half tones
hematite, Cedar Red as you
clamber
along your beechwood handle,
slip in
and out of my telephone voice.

Married to liquid spirits, ochres
and human impulse, you are
the earth's hair
releasing the sea's foamy white
escapees,
keeping the hand
moving. When did I
cross into the room
of the soul's image
to wander between
conceit and surface,
a little red *Sorry We Missed You*
on the mat.

Paintbrush, cross-body lead me
between ladder and kettle
for Robert Tressell.
Open the stone eyelids
of history, binding visions
of ghosts still alive
to the blood of Caine's tree,
on a three-pronged trident
and snare net, the upholstery
of a midnight blue limousine,
the Lorraine Hotel balcony,
teaspoon scraped into a cup

and at the feet of that boy
on cobblestones where
all roads meet Bedford Park:
Denis Law heading a goal
one hundred yards from
the colour card in monochrome –
Batman and Robin ...
'Hands that do dishes'...
Double Your Money.
Paintbrush, the revolution
will not be brought to you
by DIY SOS, door chimes
with 150 tunes including *Oh Susana*
or some i-Phone 3D robot fantasy –
gaming enough points
by the end of your life
to move onto the next game.

Paint brush of impossibly pink
uterus, pullulating
abdomen and cradle. I search
for my body's river; find drought
-cracked plaster, dermis dust
and peeling paint like ticker tape,
a light depression at the temples,
wrinkles migrating between faces
I disown, create. Paint brush,

nothing is left of me
but your exile,
a windmill without vanes
on Segar's Lane,
you take to the air
without moving, transcend all
dualities: you and me, before
and after, the writer written.
Paint brush, we face the onslaught

as one. The Rose Garden Café
overrun with rats. The aftershock
of Brexit, Covid, Big-tech – they
can virtually hoover the Louvre.

Paint brush, you outlive the hand
that sets you free. Supple
as a shielding foal inside your
bristled stock, I replenish myself.

1.5 Metres of Earth

Press-ups, sit-ups, at seven,
walled in radio words.
Martha Kearney quizzing
the oxymoronic health
minister and his mirrored
twin, a corporate vampire,
on virus guidelines and PPE.

The ceiling bites the wall
the wall bites the ceiling
and crawls under my skin
as I lie on my back, knees bent
raising my hips in the air,
lifting one leg at a time,
mask to mask with my own soul.

Is it a punishment or a gift?

It is possible I'm still alive,
paint on my face and glasses,
a raider of the lost art
climbing into the attic
lifting the rafters like Atlas,
a refugee cloud adrift between
neighbourhood stars, gimleted
by their obsolescent sculptures –
a paw here, a wing there, a dog,
a hare, 'the sisters' interminably
clear of the bull, the great whale
beneath the good ship. They see
themselves from my crow's nest.

It's hard to know what normal is

                    bending double... shouting
                    into the doctor's outdoor mic
                    chasing up the medication –
                    'The chemist says it doesn't exist' –
                    wearing a green gingham mask
                    found wrapped around the book
                    of Jeremiah in a cellophane bag
                    snagged on a railing spike.

                    Should I be indoors or out?

What is the shape of a deep sleep
or illness, the stopping of time?
I feel like my own ghost
following myself about.
Is it a punishment or gift?
They've rescued a Rescue
St Bernard from Scafell Pike.

It's hard to know what normal is

                    in shamanic flight to the ones
                    my existence depends on: maybe
                    they're here already,
                    the dead who are not dead, energy
                    between us we rarely see
                    or feel like a masked ball
                    in a secret room that contains
                    all masked balls in all secret rooms.
                    We must reinvent a face
                    for ourselves without the wrinkles
                    from that face. Closing my eyes,
                    I open them inside whose eyes?
                    Bore an escape tunnel of words
                    in this room dwarfed by this room.

                              *

What is the shape of a rupture?

George Floyd's voice. Police
seizing *I can't breathe*
masks. The Illegible blanks
of the past in each of us.

A woman's broken walk, head
-to-toe in dust and blood,
even her nightmares are under siege,
on a street of crushed cars and birds,
spikes of covid in crowded shelters.

Kids in the park by the chilling
morgue trucks of New York,
faint spray-paint: 'Dead Inside.'

Arms-length protests, candlelit vigils,
where only the dogs are gods,
sniffing amidst the chestnut leaves
that turn like pancakes on gap-toothed
shopfronts that are no longer shopfronts.

Who do I talk to when I talk to myself?

This morning it was Albert Camus
eulogizing Klopp's *Gengenpressing*
strategy at Liverpool and Moby Dick.
*There's a thin line between whaling
and attention seeking behaviour.*
I tap the keyboard, letters vanish. Albert
says his total absence is 'entirely trees'
as they communicate, share nutrients
in the mycorrhizal underground, absorb,
deflect, aerodynamic force throughout
the canopy. We're going forest bathing
with Bear Grylls, to strengthen our killer
cell function in the chemical elements
trees release.

Is it too early to heal?

Two women masked in Envy handbags,
a stack of green notes on a palm by the till.
Rainbows in the window of Venetian Blind
on Chesterfield Road where Andy Viper
the *Streak-Free* window wiper appears
dressed in silhouette and the mask of Zorro.
Hot Mushroom pie and a touch of nutmeg
in The Incredible Nutshell. *Now you know
what 1.5 metres looks like.* Christ's entry
into the Halifax, a woman in blue, haltingly
greets him holding a tray of Ferrero Rocher,
a 'suit' on his knees, screwdriver in hand
mending the safety information stand
and in the Sheaf View pub one lass's mask
sports a penis for a nose, a works night out
come-round-back barbecue in the air.
I have wings of ink and a wandering ear...
*Is it ethical to kill animals when an octopus
can open a jam jar?... I'll have another half
of that bitter, Donald, thanks.*

*

What is the shape of a rupture?

Time dissolving into place. The sun
printing images on the retina.
This city, a glockenspiel in a skip
played by hailstone, a peacock's tail
of in-your-face turquoise eyes,
bandaged words that think aloud.
Stand on the Line
1.5 Metres

This city: *Are you lost mate?*
Some kid space-walking
on the moon, wearing a head-set
in his front room. Anyone
who isn't unplugged, potentially
an agent. *This is the time*
to be slow
1.5 Metres

This city of mournful laughter,
the doors of its pubs and gyms
closing, the mask of a childlike
smile, un-slipping today
on a one-time ballerina who
kissed Rudolph Nureyev, trading
prints and verse in Tudor Square.
This is the least we can do
1.5 Metres

This city of depth-charge recall.
Opening night, a moment alone
running lines in the green room
before walking to the wing,
taking to the stage as unheeded
Cassandra or accursed Oedipus
on an islet off an island, swarm
of words rising to the throat
without a Queen. I can't breathe.
All you need is
a social worker and two doctors.
1.5 Metres

This city: a guest appearance
in the dreams of other cities
singing Nkosi Sikelel' iAfrika
in the Sheffield Trades and Social Club
Can you smell the dumplings?
I.5 Metres

The Anfield Kop, Copenhagen,
Valparaiso. *Sorry about the bin 1.5 Metres*
Havana y La Plaza de la Soledad,
Babylon, Glasgow and the Tower
of Babel. *We're here for you.*
You be here for us. 1.5 Metres

This city,
written as it writes on the body
with a crow's bile,
yelling at 'Alexa' in the garage
-converted bar, its moon
ageing without tears,
its cats playing musical stares
in the dark. The school kids
on Greta's Save Our World
demo: *There's no planet 'B'*
parents waiting in S.U.Vs, park
'disabled' outside the library
in earshot of a chanting wind
Can You Hear United Sing?
Ghost tribes of reflections, 2.15 pm
on a phantom match day.
The nomadic soul, bodies
of my body from St George's Hill
to the purloined revolution of form
and time, from bones of production
to surplus value; this city, 2.15 pm,
Can You Hear United Sing?
Maybe this is happening in a lab.

You're nearly there!

Sheffield, the world, 1.5 metres
square, a man slumped against
the glass façade of the Halifax,
rocking back and forth, talking
to himself, collapsing on his side
rocking back and forth, talking
to himself, collapsing on his side
Now you known what
1.5 metres looks like.

We reinvent signs, re-connect time
with place, the rhythms and cycles of the year
with Low Edges, Stoney Middleton, Hull
on a day break. Click, press, swipe, tick our way
back into ourselves in a whirlwind of pronouns,
receiving our other 'I' from 'you', 'him', 'her',
hewn from the 'we', put on our shoes, walk out
the door, using, abusing words, bodies of names
and verbs that encircle us in riddles, clusters
of silence that envelop us in music. 'Pandemic'
becomes 'panic', your body and words, my body
and words. Dvořák's Symphony 'From the New
World', playing in the kitchen, a woman's mask
-covered voice on the Low Edges bus... *Hello?...*
Hello? A full-grown Great Dane bounces aboard,
steaming up the startled driver's anti-covid screen...
Hello?... Hello?... Hello? Ghosts emerge
from every word like singing white smoke.
Is it too early to heal?... *Hello?... Hello?... Hello?*

Notes on Time

My body is leaving me. My father walks naked along the
    staircase
landing. I am becoming myself again. Time is neither true
nor false, it's not even time. I am too old for the battleground,
too young for the massacre. I walk without moving, this present
dangling from a pause in a cage as Hegel's 'world spirit'
rides a silicon chip. What was a motion picture has become a
    still life.

Tonight, I will brush piss on the piss painting or read *This
    Sporting Life*
after press-ups, sit-ups; before running up and down the
    staircase
to *Time Out of Mind*, Dylan's talk-sing croaking, spirit-
-sick love permeating my every atom made of before and
    after. True –
time is in a coma: a girl is caught in a basketball hoop in
    Goole. Presence
and absence, youth and prime are stowaways on the same
    cloud, ground

at the border of the country within us. We are refugees on
    ground
without ground. Time is a mask without a face – *Hi Ho Silver
    Away*. Life
takes us by surprise. You, the one woken by that balloon of
    skin, present
on your left metacarpal, water-bottle leavened, punctured on
    the staircase,
only ten years into eternity – *Hi Ho Silver Away,* the Lone
    Ranger, true
as his white stallion; master of disguise and outlaw fighting, spirit
of the western frontier, trailblazing adventurer of Hegel's

world spirit.
What is the shape of time in a covid world? A feudal battleground
against a faculty skyline, corridors between cumulus, money's true-
lie on plasma screens toasting the voters. Are we done? *This is
    Your Life!* –
the Big Red Book. I didn't look like this then: I don't now!
    My staircase
images of Bridget Bardot, Joyce Grenfell, Greta Thunberg,
    present

past and present future, what might have been and may be,
    only present
potential. This lid on a scream filming itself filming Hegel's
    world spirit
at the wheel of a self-driver in Arlington dressed as a car seat.
    My staircase
carpet's threadbare geometric patterns suggest a martial
    campground,
agonistic labour. I carry your shoulder blades on my shoulder
    blades, life's
journey through the old camps: lake trout, flat bread, tyre
    smoke, true-

lies chanted, danced; ascent and descent to the Klondike water well. True-
lies – how to name and know what you cannot see and touch,
    the present
gap between yourself and your other self. Imagine a bookshelf
    door, life
beyond corridors tying my end to your beginning, Hegel's
    world spirit
to Inuit Nunangat, where we gaze at our own ghosts on
    hunting grounds
'til we reach the horizon. The Inuit need no word for poetry.
    My staircase

exercise beckons. Time is queen of snakes, stone of hearts, present
tense. I am you, we are us, climbing stair treads to the musk-ox grounds,
the tundra listens to its echo's truth: we read and write the spirit dream.

Season of Unlocking

The sun's flash, my slow-
eyelid speed,
the room, a ghostly blur.

An accordion of books stretches
into the fingers of the dead.

The neighbours rock up
in their *Ambiance*

"We're here!"

"They're here!"

The staircase I climb
is up and down
at the same time,

"We're here!"

"They're here!"

I am predator and prey,
the table I write on
is a four-legged animal called Help!
Invisible fetters tether me
to this broken backed swivel chair,
vat of pixels, stacked-up faces,
jump-cut voices, Celebrity Squares
without the celebrities.
This is your starter for ten ...

A home that is not a place
but the image of a place,
a description of time
from another point of view?

Ching and rasp of trowel
on the gable end, dad's silhouette
against an egg white sky
singing along with a radio Sinatra ...

"When I'm out on a quiet spree
fighting vainly the old ennui
and I suddenly turn and see ..."

the front page, my inky fingers,
that photograph of a naked child
running on a road with villagers
under pestle-pounding air strikes,
a petroliferous drizzle that seeks
the bone. Black clouds of stone.

I people this house. Isabel Archer
direct from the Palace of Darkness
reverie tuning her harp strings
in the box room: *Can you hear me?*

I can smell the time-stained oak
casements and horses. Imagine
evenings of flies and jaw bones,
strength feats and card games.
Freely chosen chains of words,
a greyhound abducted by extra-
terrestrials. How could Isabel live
without exile? I people this house.

Raskolnikov asking after Sonia
through my drop-down attic cover,
her crucifix swings from *his* neck
above the stair-landing's hung bulb.

I'd like to go to Scarborough
on a steam train from York.
So many fantasy shoe shops,
rebel lemons tumbling
down steep stone steps
to a prozac on-tap shoreline.
Does talking nonsense to oneself
beat talking someone else's truth?

Acoustic strings glissando
Robert Burns' *Now Whistling Winds*
as my fugitive memory moves
from room to room, stripping
the bed, timing the egg, pulling
as the postman pushes, disappearing
by the tumble dryer *He's behind you,*
re-appearing by the combi-boiler.

In the food store I forget to pick up
ten-pounds cash-back from the auto.
Help Desk's knowledge priestess
says, 'Are you all right, lovely?'
It occurs to me I'll stay in Sheffield,
eavesdrop on myself screaming:

You're all living in a dream …

Barbra missing the Bingo on Flat Street,
and her foot massages: *I feel your*
struggle today; Barbra. I feel you
growing a little stronger at this moment,
everything closing down, I bought my
son's cot from John Lewis. Everywhere I go
in the house, I see John Lewis, my kettle,
the pick of the Maxis in a mint velvet range ...

I was told not to look back, I'm always
turning round. Is it patriarchy or cellulite?
Sue asks therapist Heather at the GP above
the library. Gives *old un* next door a shave
knowing how John, rest his soul, loved her
glide and breeze. He tells me dinosaurs
are living in his knees.

The space around me is next of kin.
I am a sieve of time within time,
previous and subsequent presents,
nameless spaces within places,
corrugated ocean, caravan of wind
bursting through me and I'm freed ...

a fresh-faced boy, stetson bobbing on his
back as he leaps through yellow ears
of wild grass towards a sun dark livery loft,
fibonacci spirals of stable dust, tumbleweed.

Depopulated glances of the city streets.
Talking to the bus stop I talk to whom?
Glass doors open and close, air enters
and leaves, conversing with itself.
A fountain made in the shape
of a pause, a little time splashes my eye.

Here on the road that goes neither way
Uma Thurman from *Pulp Fiction*
with her white Boyfriend shirt, black bob
with bangs and *Fuck the Tories* earrings
smoking a Lucky Strike by Taylor Made
here on the road that goes neither way.

> Between the vixen rouging gunnel mist
> and the badger's living-statue stare,
> Mother Hekate cultivates polytunnels
> on derelict allotments at Whitely Woods
> and Cassandra resists covid evictions
> on Rustlings Road. I steal from the dead,
> visions they had no words for when alive,
> re-make myself blood-beat by bone-flute,
> echoes in darkness. I people this house.

Gatsby asking where I'm from,
Old Sport, his pleated white cuff
reaching for her lips' touch
on his shoulder, wicker of settee
squeaking, her Mint Julep cocktail
spilling on his pant thigh, a waltz
carrying through French windows.

> How do you choose the moment to turn?
> Dogged by the stress of the halted
> reunion, I call through the letter box:
> *Eurydice, it's time to choose your eyes.*
> *Do you remember the word for lyre?*
> *'Lottie?' – the Shire mare at the park farm*
> *has foaled! They call for a name. Eurydice ...?*

You had to bend your face back
above mine, aglow from the wild flowers
over earth's edge. One breath I wanted,
a single glance of sun flushed meadow,
the agglomerate fragrance. I could have
borne the jeopardy. I people this house:

> a *here* that was another *here*, where
> a tree once caught its breath, where
> a downwardly-mobile god step-danced
> in clogs. Season of unlocking, snow
> like fat on the door mat, blood crackling
> like the sun's calligraphy in the receiver:
> *Why is a frog jumping into my kitchen?*

> *Come and have tea in our garden!*

Is this my city emerging from lockdown
or a duplicate? Singing swallows return
from a night out. I turn the day's page,
draw letters, invent a face for myself, my
hair is not my own. I look like Cousin Itt!

If you must know, all I said to Eurydice
was, 'I keep reciting the lyric I wrote you.'

> *Oh that masterpiece, I must hear it now!*
> I turn, words weigh as much as air,
> silence.
> I plant them, they grow, play dead.

Knitting Witch

This is a man who resembles Monty of Alamein, David Niven,
Alec Guinness as Charles the first in *Cromwell*. This is a man
who never lost his head, lapping the garden one hundred times
to the snare and kick of an honorary guard. This is a double,
a doppelganger, his sister's brother, a man who could turn his
walking frame into fire and ash by tossing it into the air.
This is a man in the role of Captain Tom, the river of her hands
lighting his cigarette under the mosquito net. This is a doll
of Captain Tom by Knittingwitch UK. The tabloid's poppy seed,
and horse sense for a world in agony, a palimpsest of footprints
in search of clarity across a double page of loam, mask on mask
ripening in the foliage. A puppy, foal, rescue power boat, named
after him. About turning by the phantom of his daughter's swing,
this is a man written in a mirage's light, letting the dinosaur out.

The Sheaf View

I got out of bed
on my wrong left leg ...
Where do they come from
these words? *I've been in*
a Lamborghini, I wouldn't
have one given me ...

... There's something
special about her spoons.

Idle talk sinking
in circles of creamy foam.
Submarine sentences
                        surfacing –

You wouldn't
        go out of your way
        to kill an ant
but if it trespassed
            on your project,
        you'd just react.
        We are the ants.

Where do they come from
these voices
that echo like an iris
reflected in an iris, words
that fall from the steps
of a star into all the other
nights within this one.

The dialogue
    between a violin
        and a disjointed
        murmur
to my left.

The old-time gardeners
weeding tabloid papers
round the corner table.

Walter easing his out-
of-kilter spine
that *went completely
this morning*, up and down
an oaken post, nodding his
head like a dashboard dog
to earphone music, bending
knees – soon to be replaced –
on the down stroke.

The *Red* tree surgeons of
the great leap forward.
The target-driven florists,
teachers, printmakers,
pet groomers of the full
treatment, film students
who film students, DJs,
and unsung band players
eclipsed by the language
that hails them.
*Have you heard
Five Square Yards
        of Blackness?*
  They're on
        at the *Cremone*
with Twenty Foot Squid.

                    Rivulets
of condensation, a slow
motion butchery of faces
in the window night,
                    ears   wandering
       between   syllables.
Hands and lips of words
hurl themselves
between pony-tails,
book-shelves, the singing
bald-headed card-player
who's got *nowt*
              to back it up with.

Listen and you hear
your own voice
when a jar of Easy Rider
talks to a denim jacket,
a beer mat to a table top,
a bucket of suds to itself.

Our canine ghost –
              Dougal
Who Sat Round About
              Here
sniffs for a spectral pig's ear.

Mirror work mirroring
another time in time ...

ENCORE WHISKY

'*Total Pain Combatant*'

'*All Injurious*
       Substance
              Removed'

Two dogs bark at one another
pull on their leash.
Two poems tear one another
apart, a third is born
under the paper stand with
the liquid urgency of a gull
in a half-honey sky.

Do they still do Revels?

We are fluent in water,
a tongue's wine, words
erasing, creating,
an excess of beginnings
that begin again, people
becoming someone else
when they're banging
and stamping their fist
and feet, shouting...
Spritzer!...
       Spritzer!...
             Spritzer!...

Time for a man I don't know
to place a double
malt scotch
         on the table
in front of me
      because it's *his*
birthday. Draw a Queen
for a straight. Walter
to walk again,
retrieve a flow of blood,
a decrepit green cushion
with its own eco-system.

It could be the beer,
late night tiredness.
It could be the souls
of dead poets abandoning us
as Alice carries her suds,
passes *Where the Bombs fell.*

My right-hand presses hard
on my woolly-hatted head.
It's the first cold night
of the winter. Sirens chase
sirens and the joy riders
of Heeley Green.

Contagion

I see the almost empty road to the horizon
not the pavements that echo of nothing,
a yellow toddler's raincoat not the mother.
I see the 'take-it-on-the-chin' laughter
of the performative window cleaner
working that 'S' motion with his squeegee
retracing the sweep back up and round
for that minor chord of water left behind.

Tunnelled vision, a common condition
says the doctor on the phone. *How many
units of alcohol do you consume?*
What a fool I've been sat in The Guzzle
between divider screens and florid faces,
that man shouting, *I can't see. Linda,
are you there?* The woman behind the bar
comes in so close she touches his heart
with her mobile phone. *He's the third
this week*, a kind of birth, easy to mistake
for the leaving of a dream in a dream,
all the senses under siege. I must run back
climb up, jump out, it draws me in deeper.

It only takes exposure to infected words.
A bus driver plunges into a halo of fire
at the lights, a doctor reaches for, misses,
her *Fabulously Fab at 50* mug, stumbles
into herself. It happens to a woman while
eating poached salmon at The Amadeus,
a man reading, *An Invitation to The Great
Awakening in Dayton, Ohio*. Blood tests,
MRIs, CT scans, therapy, our sins exposed
to the postmodern confessor. I see with my
finger-tips what my eyes used to touch,

forget the word for chair, sounds
that can't be named for names, your voice,
what use are names to me now? Blindness
with no visible change in the eye as if I'm
in hibernation. Are you there? Is that you?

If you see me rubbing my chest and thighs
with a pebble in the jelly fish tactile rain,
keep it to yourself. They're working with
a chimpanzee and Trojan horse to be first
to the vaccine – the poem without words.
I take a glass of water to the ocean, return
with a bucket of questions, every gesture
risking attention from swivel-eyed snipers
of myopic vision, data curators, and brain-
interface scientists with a pocket wine list,
those who see others as they see themselves.

What happens to love when there is only *now*?
I reach for likeness, unlikeness, a rectangle
of opaque light. I walk through to a tree
of blurred calligraphy written by the sun.
Absence sneaks up on me from the front.
I can't make out a song's last line on the radio
for its southern vowels, repeated three times.
The daily work-out begins next door, intervals
of machine-gun footfall on the staircase.
I carry the elephant in the room on my back,
breathing like Miles Davies after his illnesses
got a grip. Who and where is the resistance?

Rest your chin here and look straight ahead,
if you see a prick of light between 'you' and 'me'
put your finger over it: trace a down-stroke,
up-curve, write the first word in the bridge
of 'us' and 'we', contours and traces of colour
coming into focus: we'll meet above the water.

All that's Solid Melts into Air

(Capitalism clearly states no other idols are to be worshiped other than the golden calf.)

She looms ever larger, losing her edge in his tangled breath
where Broadway meets the stock exchange's high reliefs,
floor traders in *futures* behind deep set windows, Washington,
the flag. Passersby strike *her* stance, arm-in-arm with fifty inches
of hollow bronze, facing up the *Wall Street Bull*. Money snorts,
bellows like a quorum of gods. *Why not call her Greta Thunberg?*
She's *more* like *Orphan Annie!* Hells bells hunkered haunches
lunge: *Fearless Girl's* open-grave stare. Who is Narcissus: who is
the mirror? Dow Jones ticking, the girl steps from herself to grab
the horns, setting fire to paper tongues, swinging herself upside-
down for the arcing spine, wheeling knees, landing feet on loin,
rump, to leap clear. *Why not call her Fearless Woman? More like
young Judy: There's no place like Wall Street.* Dow trending
down, that nostril flare, windswept skirt, tail curling like a lash.

Workout

Bass and drums split the poem,
scatter syllables like freckles.
I write on this side of my eyelids
as I plank hold: press up: blink –
a word falls into line.

Someone's left the mirrors running:
my *double* bends one knee
at a time, stretching his hamstrings,
I break the line, push myself
beyond any description
of deferred elation written in sweat,

the body is a blank page.
We work to the blood meat pulse
of muscles and voices, self-tortured,
misshapen. Dan bulks up delts
and pecs, taking note of reps and sets,
almost his own master piece.
Gemma's tattoos are a sub-titled film
now showing on her tan. Is that him –

the new man? Resisting the ego lift
stretching the resistance band,
my every word someone else's
mis-behaving child. Men and women
jump squat, dead lift, out run
a pride of not so subordinate clauses,
lactic acid flushing calves and thighs
until the body surpasses itself.
Who am I that you become my other?

The jack-knifed back leg,
sole of the foot on your head
smiling in inverted commas,
the Poem of the Day poised
between self-surrender and surrender
of a self, a fitness suite chain reaction,
a sweat stained negative left on vinyl.

Jo strides into the garden of bodies
in power-leggings and support-bra.
If you are my narcissus I am your
reflection. Have you seen my water bottle?
I listen to the echo within the echo
amidst a chaos of personal pronouns.
Whose being do I name on my knuckles?

Bass and drums split the poem
cross trainers and stair masters drift
in the force field of possible gyms.
I hang from the edge of a word
looking for clusters, creaturely signs,
clear white space for a peacock's ink
between voluntary delusion
and Gorgeous George. Blue stars leak,
core balls float. Down-dog, dead-bug
in the warm-down. Superman –
left arm, right leg, extended: left knee
grounded – beginning to stammer.
I tear this work out from my notebook.

Country of My Shadow

When I pass through the rock face what do I say to my wolf
    soul?
Who is in exile in whom? Living with lino, manila envelopes,
    the Now
Show; in and out of tree shadow, bin alley, the heritage
    picture
house, the workers' club with spring floor and velvet trim on
    Mulehouse Road,
winding shy of the sole surviving police box on Surrey Street,
    gimleted
by lamb burgers, fear and anger stealing electrons, building
    tumors under the skin.

Nothing as narrow as borderland, a wolf howl to her mate,
    skin
and fur separate, crimson glazed, my wounded wound and
    wolf soul
loping between leather soles dealing playing cards to
    flagstones, gimleted
by a three-headed sun kneeling on my neck. How we need
    Blake's child-god now,
words that shed shadows, riding the reindeer drum to the
    house
north of the interloper's compass, my body as strong as
    laughing water. Picture

me loping out of darkness's bandages to enter my other.
  Picture
Pallas Athene, Homer Simpson as Greta Thunberg amidst
  ghosts of skin-
tight hunger, where no one arrives but the stranger. The White
  House
is baiting the bear, again. My ruins lie behind and in front of
  me, soul
cornered by check points, receding borders. Kids mock the
  virus now –
I've been chasing it, fucking actively seeking it. Scatter-gun
  shoppers, gimleted

by self-isolation. It's hard to tell who's locked in from who's
  locked out, gimleted
by a virus mutating, Antigone's drag and dig pop-up burials
  coining it. Picture
a chugger chain-saw barking death and life, cages of air, now
the self-isolation choir singing 'Desolation Row,' 'You'll
  never walk alone.' Skin
ends where it begins. I travel from name to name, say to my
  wolf soul:
*Stitch the wound, tear it open, unloose me by the kidney
  garden mission house,*

(*take a rich wife!*), aware I'm more and less than myself, the
  house
trained dance mate of the irresistible tantrum on Arundel
  Gate, gimleted
by reflections uniting verb and pronoun until words impact
  and scatter. Wolf soul –
equal to my exile in withers and hackles, Mother Hecate's
  polytunnels. Picture
Persephone preparing to resist Covid evictions on Rustlings
  Road, skin
and clay, a distant blaze of eyes leaping between meanings...
  now

in a few sentences... This is your lost tongue... your host
    knows you are... now
hacked off. Goodbye John Lewis, Bamber Gascoigne. Hello
    OxyContin, the house
of oblivion. I ask who am I, out of lip synch, pronouns resolve
    into skin
and salt, you and I, we and us. My self's wolf howls in relief,
    gimleted
words click like tumblers on a safe untrusted. I carry my
    country with me, picture
shadow with the scent of garlic and blood, two strangers who
    sense a wolf soul

in their midst. Picture, the martyred tap root, Rumi's Guest
    House, gimleted
by the butterfly's lyric, the kingfisher's ink, the quartered soul
    of time, lips
and hands of wind. Now, place the cave bear's tooth in the
    vison quest niche. Howl!

One Good Eye

I rock and tear the crust,
prowl with hurricanes
in a tornado's eye, veil
the setting sun where fowls
roost at noon and orange
snow falls in July.

I laugh, forgive me, love
the name people give me –
Agua; their promise
to tend the slopes singing
my praise. I'm so close
after all to the living cell:
mineral, eloquent, family.

I have such a dry mouth.
Tongues that are pokers,
fluent as a viper's ink,
cyphers of the earth's anger
at dead lakes, trees that fall
like slain chiefs: Red Cloud,
Standing Bear, Crazy Horse.

My irradiating spears arc
and spatter, distributaries
of crimson gold sizzle
like a boiling kettle, force
bloody clots, a diaphanous
calligraphy in the dark
hinterland, a poem broken
open where it meets reality.

It's late. Experts in hazmats
dip fragments in liquid, read
the runes. Bells brain,
chapels smell of burnt tears.

They pray for an appearance,
a chance to re-negotiate
the covenant. A woman
rises breathless to hard won
feet, wearing a hat like a lid
on a scream, hobbles on her
heart past the alter. *How
would'ya like to be overthrown?*

When my smoky fingers
reach the ocean
that suffering joker
laughs like there's a tomorrow.

Who is it in my ears?
Who is it in my voice?
Is this how their dead mourn?

People, relentlessly sweep
and hose, talk to the birds,
my vomitus flow 15 feet high
stops at a zebra crossing.

Exiles write ghost stories
in the village hall. A cat
called Dorothy Fish strolls
past gobs of cold black fire
heading for the allotments.

I see it all with my one good eye.

Sabrina

Sabrina is staring
at the long blue dress
standing between tea-pots
nit-combs, a rock art boulder,
a vacuum-cleaner, waiting
on the fourth date with her
'new man,' a sports physio
who writes poetry. 'One thirty
he'll buy me a baked potato.'

How did I become her other's
other? Her poet's poet
like Pushkin's narrator, helpless
to save Tatyana and Onegin
from one another; Sabrina
from one of three, five, seven
poets between her and me,
co-writing a new elegy to past
and future ancients, no barriers
between millennia of vertebrae,
and 2,000 gods, cipher stone
and archive film, the jitterbug
and the eland bull mating-dance,
nasal blood splashing cloak hide,
the bear skull dead centre.

'There are so many things,'
Sabrina says: a hanging
plastic side of beef at George
and Joyce's Quality Butcher's,
names that teach us irony:
Freedom Road, Industry Street.
I have to tell you now... A bust

of Sam Holberry... *no such*
undertaking has been received ...
The Greenham Common Women,

> not an 'I' nor a 'you'
> but a hand-in-hand 'we,' shot
> standing round the barbed
> perimeter skyline. *Bring Mirrors*
> *Turn the Commons Upside Down.*
> I am re-born ...

iamb, trochee, trampled moments,
lightning flashes in cross rhythms
of slippage; receiving my other 'I'
entering and leaving me like exile.
.

> As a child I awoke in the night
> took a fork and popped a blister
> like a golf-ball on my hand's heel
> where the rubber bottle had scalded
> and reaching for the light-switch,
> caught sight of my soul's image
> by the armchair with antimacassar –
> a still present passing past, resisting
> return from that dormant TV screen.
> *Have you lived seven of my years?*

'Can you take photographs?'
Sabrina asks, entering *Spirit*
of Sheffield. We give each other eyes.
Leaves are rising to branches. They're
taking down steel and putting up
timber roofing at the railway station.

> I can't see for deafening darkness,
> white smoke, a hand waving,
> a farmer on a horse-drawn plough,

a woman in a long blue dress
standing under the hanging-clock.
Walking down Hard Up Street 'n'
Canned Up Street for the matinee,
chips from Chippingham's chippy,
nude fan dancing at the Palace.

They shift fans about, love
tha couldn't see owt,
they're fully clothed underneath.
The comedian was vulgar, George.
Don't you dare take me there again.

Sabrina, interested in the evolution
of design and archaeological finds,
loves the Bronze Age Roundhouse
they built to greet the morning sun.

Actual straw, actual wood,
this will be mud: it's home!

I'll make the flames...
You make the flames
and I'll get my hat...

You've fire in your belly!

I've fire in my hat...

No! Not in your hat
it's not big enough!

When do the clothes we wear
become costumes
and the things we do
re-enactments?

Kids building pyramids
with wood blocks,
stiff-limbed zombie-walking
out of *Ancient Egypt*
as if pulling against bandage;
teacher dressed as Nefertiti,
Walk Dylan, sensibly, please.

Sabrina, enthralled by the statuette
of a cat goddess, talks as if she
has a companion. I'd like to return
like Peter Falk in *Wings of Desire*:
'I can't see ya, but I know you're here'

Who is overflowing who?
She is neither the wound's echo
nor the echo's wound,
the thawing mirror
nor the antlers floating like branches.
I'm not the person I was
when I got off the bus.
'That doll's house creeps me out.'
That's life...
that's what all the people say,
You're riding high in April,
shot down in May...

'What will they find of us?'
Sabrina asks. Not the hard drive
illegible to tomorrow's technologies
but bubble gum and marriage status,
knee and hip replacements,
sealed in silt. Epidemics of willing
blindness. Talking heads looping on
ad infinitum in *Beneath Our Feet*.
The words of three, five, seven, poets
between her and me, co-writing a new

elegy to mother clay, dug-up rage,
squinting alphabets, spirit animals,
the painted that is the real human-lion.
A mirage we inhabit that only a child's
Buddha mind could penetrate.
You have to eat me now dad.
The mandible of Sabrina's 'new man':
somebody else's somebody else
bringing everybody back.

Mummy look!

Ooh, what's Charlotte found, Danny?

A baby chimpanzee!

*It looks like a peacock, sweetheart.
Don't knock, they're dead.*

Are we dead?

*Don't be silly, Danny
Now, what have you found?*

A baby chimpanzee!

Through the Wall

Human as a wheel, heat shrunk,
a moment of risk when the work
of carpenter or smith could be spoilt.
Human as a voice at the edge
of a smoke-drunk woodland,
out-of-body travel, the desire of dust
to breathe, light to be something else –
blue-glass bead seniority or serenity,
an alphabet, a hairpin, a vision quest.
Human as the Statute of Incantation,
an excess of absence, abandonment
between foresight and after-thought,
'no-where' and 'here-ness,'
'no-when' and 'now-ness,'
I can tell you this because you, like me,
are poised between birth pain
and grave goods, half-oblivion
and half-memory, stampeding ghosts
and conflicted Persephone.

Why do we believe they can help us?
The dead and the living, eyes that blink
on both sides of time's aquarium:
climbing fish, Short-Faced Bear,
Giant Penguin and Anglo-Saxon,
I can ask you this because you, like me,
tumble hoof-over-muzzle in the vortex,
incant the rock and goat trail
to the six-lane highway with no exit,
the dead and the sleeping, so alike.

Human as full handprints, blow-sealed
on the rock face in a hematite-red haze –
that crooked little-finger –
sometimes they won't let us through.
Human as the aged Shire-mare's halter,
encrusted with rawhide and salt foam,
hanging behind the stable door.
Human as a bare-foot duchess's first
jaunt out with butterfly net
and the raffish lepidopterist.

That night the dog flew into a frenzy
clamping his jaws on pyjama leggings,
dragging blankets off the bed, minutes
before the bomb hit the street
behind our street. I can tell you this
because you, like me, are infinite,
of the same calcite as bone flutes,
and subways, the inner-ear – poised
between torment and music.
Human as a harpsichord of footsteps,
human as souls who travel in relics,
do you turn to the Talking Skull,
learn the tongue of the tongue-less one?
'What do you know about life
and death?' Now residing in the chest
o' drawers lined with a Liverpool
v Swansea *Daily Mirror* match report.

One day I will become what I want –
a stonechat, a stone chair, a shaman
with a dry mouth in a battered canoe
passing through the wall bird-footed,
returning brand-suited, a consultant
of dysfunction with a horse's head,
anything to draw an audience, jump
clean-hoofed into the listening-dark,
landing in the canter of the poem,
human as your and my stranger-self,
the untold truths of the dead,
and the living who dig for light.

The Great Plains

I just can't cry I tell you why
It's the way I lie on my back
under the brow of the moon
open to the plains
on my side I fall like a page
wrapped round a stone
last night's word Whereas
for poet Layla Long Soldier
of the Oglala Lakota
who defeated Custer
'tree' is tonight's word
tonight's word is 'tear'
but when I write 'tear'
the word 'tree' appears
I just can't cry
I'll tell you why
it's the way I lie
the lightbulb hangs by a tear
who is she for whom I wait
from dust to grape we dance
her small instep kicking up
leaves like pancakes
if poems require words lying
on my back that's the default
the continuum it's not a state
of learning of thinking muscles
speak pages are bodies branches
in motion syllables sound
I just can't cry I'll tell you why
Let them eat grass
one trader said they found him
with grass in his mouth
on my back I see the blue tear

of a gas lit flame a salt cellar
spilling white crystals on brown
wrapping paper darkness
is a concept silence is laughter
there's light on the plains
lying on my right side
the big screen of my third eye is dark
but on my back the stars weep solder
point weld road signs jalopies on bricks
in the driveways of childhood
Granma Forbes pushing at the rear
of her grandson's car
till the exhaust pipe falls in the road
lying on my right side
Play the meter reading wheel of fortune
You've earned a free spin
Lying on my back I move my mouth
as if talking someone down blink
an eye tenses change syllables sound
a white horse looks at a white horse
the colors of molten steel
are jealous of the dusking sky
on the Great Plains the wind breathes
on my face I don't know whether I'm
the ventriloquized or the ventriloquist
I just can't cry I'll tell you why
when I lie on my side one eye open
to the firescape but on my back
I am the dreamer and the dream
that everyone returns
when I lie on my back
open to the plains I just can't cry

Carrying a Tree on the Bus to Low Edges

hot-house eyes of the driver,
tributaries branching across the aisle.
Eyes, leaves, cheek bones,
a spider's web tattoo around a neck,
the Tom Jones *Sex Bomb* ring tone,
I feel them enter the vibrating web.
A green patina spreads like memory
across my skin. 'Sorry
you must say *sorry*, you catch this lady
with your twig...' I scream
below some imperceptible threshold
as if anchored in the canal,
not yet born, in another tense or field,
carrying a tree on the bus to Low Edges.
The lake is drowning in concrete,
the forest goes by so quickly,
has someone thrown a switch. 'Sorry
you must say sorry and do up your zip –
you embarrass the bus.'
Who is taking whom to where.
I am not on a journey: I am the journey.

*

Passengers google i-Phones ...
*Does Botox hurt... How tall
is John Travolta... Dangers
of woodworm in windmill restoration ...*
I shed a nut, a nose grows longer,
wrinkles crawl from face
to face, I can't dissociate
bark and skin, tense
and pronoun, leaf

and hair. They name me Sylvatica, one
who returns like Persephone.
Who wouldn't be a tree again.
I migrate across the shadow grey
of the white roof-line
above vociferous trumpets,
hardy perennials, a gardenia from Basra.
Dark-green surges, my heart pumping
sap. There is this person inside of me.
I think I could lose him in traffic.

                    *

In the 80's, it was five pence
per journey, tree or no tree.
Have you heard of the Hoochie Pincohie,
where I dip my ankle
and campgrounds worship
on the grass of my shadow,
a cleansing, resin-scented, canopy
edible before the storm
becomes the storm. What will the ice-core,
bone-scan, depth-sound, updates
of the committee tell us. 'Excuse me,
is that the bible you're reading?'
'No!'
'What is it?'
'Not the bible'
'Sorry... it's my turn to say sorry...
I've annoyed myself since I was twelve...
My mother took me to school.'

                    *

A woman's laughter weeps,
her bulldog panting clouds,
her man shambling down the aisle
like a stoned llama with three legs.
They know we're out of time.
They can't help it. Can they help it.
Where is the woman who sings
What a friend we have in Jesus.
'Come now you can sing it with me.'

*

Is to move like a cloud of birds,
the blue of the sea, a tree on the bus,
elegy or prophecy... *Burger Buzz,*
derma flow, Beds and Mattresses
where the *Vietnamese Café* meets
Mother Hubbard's new chippy,
Airy Fairy... Tea With Percie...
as if names sing life in and out of places,
turn a butcher's into a nursery garden,
carry a tree on the bus to Low Edges.

*

A flashbulb sun publishes offshoots
on foreheads, a gleaming bald head,
a narrative gap in the teeth, figures
tightly wrapped, involutions
edged crimson and pink,
a leopard print headscarf, blur
of pigeon, glimpse
of the gilded golden taxi cab
on the roof of *Mr Compensator.*
Even the context is out of context.
I shed a nut. Where is the man who
speaks into his dud i-Phone

about daring heists, running the wing.
The chassis rattles and shudders,
the engine snores. No.
It's me shuddering,
it's the driver snoring.
Where are the velvet curtains,
the usherette with ices,
we need an intermission.
Is 'love' the destination... Lidl...
... the lake of fractured bone ...
the queue for the checkout till,
voting booth or open mic.
Where's the woman who sings 'Strange Fruit'
to the lower deck.
'Come now you can sing it with me.'

*

I am moved but feel I'm standing still.
This would be a good time to take root,
climb my rung-less ladder
abolish the horseless milk float
refurbish the shipwrecked bus fleet.
Don't take my word for it,
look at the skips in the street.
Press this bell and the bus will slow.
Small ones know their dinosaurs, you know.
They say it all the time... 'You know'
What is it they know.

*

City ambassadors with the blood of peacocks,
football fans chanting 'You're just a man
with a jacket' to a man in a jacket
on the door of the Globe along the city gateway,
a hopping wagtail's epic passage.

Will you carry me if I carry you.
The sea and the desert are mine,
the hawk's banner and the rain's guitar are mine.
I am and am not mine.
Where's the woman who sings 'I put a spell on you'
to the lower deck.
All the roads are knotting up,
eyes and leaves detach like tears.
Am I bleeding or sweating
are they singing or screaming.
A man wired as a hive of diligent bees,
shouts, 'Twenty-first century people are stupid.'
A full-headed Dahlia puts on her eyes.
Is the future listening like the dead.
I can touch its grief.
Licking flares on the horizon,
drowning water-tanks and wells.
Here, shadows stoop like question marks
at petrol pumps, move
as if moments, days, are in them,
looking for direction... alibi, metaphor.
Why tea lights are so called?
How to style curtain bangs?
Will there be islands.
The horizon is dissolving.
Will the sky be visible from Low Edges,
the weather is their religion. Look...
two young ravens take it in turn to cross-body lead
in a gateless field.
What is coming.
Will you be there.
They can't hear me.
Can they hear me.
Are you their other image.
A wild boar squeezes brown sauce on a pork pie
in a window seat. Will there be outposts on stars
that resemble Great Egrets in breeding plumage.

I can no longer see the Three Witches.
Magic words vibrate the spider's web, string
by string, 'Sometimes I go dizzy, see black spots ...
you've got to laugh.'
'Why?'

*

They know I'm in here.
Do they occupy, trespass, prosecute ...
sentence.
When I move I'm target light.
They're teaching me manners today.
How to say sorry.

Ode to a Donkey Jacket

I hang you on the door frame.
You look at me
through button-holes.
DJ of night-shifts, half-
bricks at the crack
of a trowel, adhesive paste
daubed on a hammer shaft
for a laugh. DJ, my northern
over-soul, if you were
to unbutton my skin
you'd find a child, a donkey
engine, a vintage navy *Wool
Mix,* unisex, council approved,
vinegared chips, a navigator
of sun-blind corridors, a spiral
staircase to the skywalk
estate, the half-buried ribcage
of an etherized god. *Don't worry
this isn't for you...* hammer-
in-hand swinging low,
before the tower-block quakes,
a door goes through.
Unpindownable to one locker
room, picket line, name, you
marched to ban the 'H-bomb':
the world is a severed head
with best salon facial.
They're programming humans
to think like humans:
it's futile, for it is you, DJ, who
is the fully sensuous wool mix,
a definite quantity of necessary
social labour, the material

foundation and guiding thread
of concept fashion. I'll give you
catwalk trauma, picket line chic,
by way of road blocks, Orgreave,
army and police. DJ,
you are the in-and-for-yourself
frenzy of immediate action,
the negation of Eton twill
and Oxford cloth, as obdurate
as body water, pumice smooth,
arriving in your original box
(due to missing items no longer
posted to Twickenham). DJ,
you could not be more beautiful
if a hurricane carries you
to Rosa Luxemburg's speech
at the *Hanover Conference* –
'Manure is the soul of agriculture' –
if your pocket crumpled receipt
read: Bananas Loose.
LG PK Beetroot. DJ,
does my sweep mean anything
to you when I brush split-hairs
off your shoulders, suture your
tartan lining, armpit to armpit
torn, with a swarm of needles.
I dip my pen in your still fresh
wound. A horn blows, workers
remove their hard hats. Words
pour down your sleeve
on to my page, arrest the sun
with an unconscious hand.
DJ, if you found yourself
under my skin, would you itch?

Nocturne

Night of a sea's insomnia.
Night of the cross-body lead
by the Budding Picassos Ceramic Café.

Night of eyes that close
open inside my eyes. Somebody beside me
moves the pen while the blood

comes and goes. Night that doesn't talk, it says –
'The dead are not dead
they are spiritual liaison officers, the living step

on air and jar themselves.'
Night of hidden bones, broken springs, skips
and stars. Night of the less credible bus-shelter,

Luxury Nails upside down among floating leaves.
Is it you, me, pigeon guano under the bridge
or the laughter that goes both ways?

Night of the sky falling up, slinkies of darkness.
I leave myself, return, leave myself. It's semi-true.
Night of tribes and dialects of silhouette,

the endangered red-tailed black shark gable-end
stencilled-in-darkness, lamp posts pulled down
by the moon. Night, a doorway's scream

rushes my heart, a woman waits for toasted cheese,
warming her hands on the silver urn. Night, nouns
become verbs, pronouns dissolve, foothills erode.

Let us rebuild the pyramids in Low Edges
before Phillip Marlowe arrives home to the cat
and two solitudes enter a higher intensity.

Is this your self-portrait or mine? Night
of the *greater-than* arrow-head on the road side
driving us to words, weeds, non-sequiturs,

realpolitik, Britain's Got Amnesia. Night, lost
in bottle caps and Newkie Brown, wrinkles
and eyebrows migrating across cheekbones

and foreheads, Ivor Cutler drinking with Agrippina,
Fidel Castro playing the one-armed bandit.
Now the 'No-Me' meets the 'No-I'. Where are you?

Are you? Night that gazes at eyes that mirror
my eyes into which you gaze at a negative –
leaf or leaves, twig or tree, an octopus earnestly,

endlessly changing its form or me. I lower
my bucket of light into your sediment, wait
for chiaroscuro shapes to fix where you remain,

unwilling to accede, be still, readable.

Tubar Mirabilis

I'm reading *Two Guitars*
thinking of the space between notes.
John Cage said he'd devote his life
to beating his head against the wall.
I've just about reached singing point ...
1,2,3,4... 1,2,3,4,5,6... 1,2,3,4,5,6,7,8...

You make me feel like a paddle board
You make me feel like a paddle board
You make me feel like a paddle board
instructor teaching people to walk on
walk on walk on water in the Albert Hall ...
1,2,3,4... 1,2,3,4,5,6... 1,2,3,4,5,6,7,8...

I feel like the silence between footsteps,
a sculpture of air.
Is 'Those Days Are Gone' a rip-off
from Rachmaninov? I curse the jazz
at the University Arms, worship
the tom toms of gutter rain drumming
on the asphalt roof of my window bay
because Ellington is not an Avenue,
Leonard Cohen is no cul-de-sac.
I circle vultures, crash the organ
in the Albert Hall to still energy: 9,999
pipes from the size of a drinking straw
to a factory chimney, take a sip, look
at me, dead and alive, 'Einstein
on the Beach,' a perfect disguise, a knot
of tenses in the 'court-trial', 'space-ship,'
'night-train'. I hold my harmonica out
of the window, wait on the speed change,
it's so simple, there's so much to play.

Are these the days my friends?
1,2,3,4... 1,2,3,4,5,6... 1,2,3,4,5,6,7,8...

You make me feel like a paddle board
sellotaped with string
You make me feel like a paddle board
sellotaped with string
I must put this poem to music before it
questions the I Ching
1,2,3,4... 1,2,3,4,5,6... 1,2,3,4,5,6,7,8...

A body hears a body and answers with
a question. I feel like the space
between notes, stapled by habit,
instinct, Dionysus and paranoia,
these are all the days my friends.
1,2,3,4... 1,2,3,4,5,6... 1,2,3,4, 5,6,7,8...

I was hit on the head by a dead owl
falling like a feathery rock
I was hit on the head by a dead owl
falling like a feathery rock.

What is it that takes over, don't say
not either or but feeling
and form, the recycled trombone
urinals of Freiburg and Ticehurst,
bubbles and burn, 'Some of These Days'
1,2,3,4... 2,3,4,5... 3,4,5,6... 4,5,6,7...

It's midnight at the Oasis
I've sent my camel to bed
It's midnight at the Oasis
I've sent my camel to bed

Are *Six Pianos* the same
as *Six Marimbas*? If only it were seven.

I feel like *4′33″* of throat clearing,
breath stirring a blank sheet of paper,
connoisseurs walking back in the hall –
a faint sharp horn – to walk out again.
It's not what it is: it's what is it. Cage
visited an anechoic chamber. Duchamp
asked him if he was alright. Cage
visited an anechoic chamber. Duchamp
urged him to be a magnet not a skip
a magnet not a skip, soloing ...1,2,3,4,5, ...
2,3,4,5,6... 3,4,5,6,7... 4,5,6,7,8...
If I could make music for the people
bending notes, timing time
under the rib cage and out on the street
in a country where only the mist is real.
Well, these are all the days my friends.
4,3,2,1... 5,4,3,2... 6,5,4,3...7,6,5,4...

I'm working on the twelve-tone staircase
breathless slide-stepping half-naked
I'm working on the twelve-tone staircase
1 and 2 and 3 and 4... 2 and 3 and 4
and 5... 3 and 4 and 5 and 6... 4 and 5
and 6 and 7... 5 and 6 and 7 and 8...
Are all these days the days my friends?

To anyone who isn't now confused
my question is. Does it never stop?
Is sound enough? Squeaky bin bags,
distant hoovers, Martha's unfelted
steps to the stops and pipes, raising
her wooden broom for a mic to sing

Crazy,
I'm crazy for feeling so lonely. I'm
crazy,
crazy for feeling so blue...

to her morning after comrade cleaners
in their tabard aprons. Martha's voice
like fits of rain suturing the emptiness,
her hands still wet in plastic gloves.
And these are all of the days my friends.
1,2,3,4... 1,2,3,4,5,6... 1,2,3,4,5,6,7,8...

An alto sax is breaking up a molecule,
I'm flung out of my own skin.
There are no safety belts on Jupiter,
pencils wedged between the keys,
no-thing and the beat hold them in –
Jupiter can be delicate –
How to Train your Dragon after Bach.
1,2,3,4...1,2,3,4,5,6... 1,2,3,4,5,6,7,8...
1,2,3,4... 1,2,3,4,5,6... 1,2,3,4,5,6,7,8...
1,2,3,4...1,2,3,4,5,6... 1,2,3,4,5,6,7,8...

Ghosted

We swing our feet in chestnut leaves that drift
  like spotted eagle-rays, a half-brick
in my jacket pocket, your stalker for life on our trail.
  Twenty-six years later I find you in the fridge.
You drive a slice of toast through my heart.
  Does it matter if you're not who you are
as long as one of us loves the other? I find you
  in the panelled door I gloss with the sable brush
my father gave me, now fifty years old. Whose skin
  is this I touch? I am not you, I am not
not you. Why worry if love and hate
  are a two-personned god if someone else
who looks like you is with me now. We laugh
  in separate centuries, I'm still laughing at the self-
playing piano, your joke about the man who
  asks the barber for 'a Leo Sayer.' You give me
new buttocks put my body together. I sculpt
  the nape of your neck with the heel of my thumb
singing Marlene Dietrich's *Falling in Love Again*,
  my vowels as long as a Mother Superior's cornet.
We are connected by static: what I said sounded like
  a yawn and you said was a gradual breathing out,
we are connected by passport, wetsuit, cagoule,
  You Want It Darker, tea bags, Henderson's Relish,
lists you love. We are connected by red velvet
  drapes that separate traffic from the café
with the cine in the cellar showing Nicole and Tom
in *Eyes Wide Shut.* We are connected by the method
  of dab, dots of colour fusing in the viewer's eyes,
you exceed yourself become your other 'I':
  the figurine at the Lieberghaus with the bum

'I want and want now,' argue with staff as I'm body-
      checked where lacquered Buddha's smile
like TV quiz show hosts. What shall I be after you?
      The moving image that doesn't move
in Filmmuseum Düsseldorf now showing the third,
      fifth and seventh of us between you,
and Marlene's 'illusion' gown of strategic sequins
      and pain: *What am I to do.*
Watch two bodies become one in your eyes – a thigh,
      fingers, hair, the lamp-shade, the slow-pan
to the spider's web, linen chest, the leopard cub
      meticulously licking its paws as you enter my
voice through the rib cage, a song I forget to forget.
      Is everything that consoles fake? Remember our
impromptu escape through the function suite car park
      of the Crown Hotel? Your stalker for life
on our trail. You make the film: I'll write the poem.
      Can you see my true lies
dissolve halfway across the unwritten horizon
      and all the more beautiful for that.
I know you won't disappoint me.

Monsoon

Listen to the first drops scissor
cutting round the gable end.
The rain on my shoulder
chooses its own exile,
I choose my own rain.

I've

    not

                    been
myself

    since
            it

                    rained
        in
            my

head

            Are we extinct yet.
        There's a bear people think
            is dressed up as a bear
    and a zoo of costumed humans.
        I'm hanging in the balance,
        a salmon swims through me.

I've

                not

been

        myself
                since
            it

    rained

                in

my

                head

I don't fit in my own dream
says the spinning earth
tempted to stop
suddenly –
autocorrected
soddenly. Where are the birds.
The Doomsday Clock ticks
forward two seconds,
I pick up the receiver –
Remember me? says the rain.
How can you refuse
to be part of it and avoid
being alone. People hold
the rods steadily – envision.
You do have a plan?
asks the rain. We can...

can we live beneath
earth's skin, find paradise over
-thrown, Bel-Air mansion rents
in Sandy Springs. How easy it is
to kill a river, blood ink running
thin, fear dries the mouth,
meaning rushes in. Is it too late
to talk of the groundwater re
-charge. I don't want
this poem to die of thirst.

I've

not

been

myself

since

it

rained

in

my

head

Rain of ancient smoke,
raw milk, my own ghost
laughing at its double
exposure in the window
of *Patriot Games* once *Housing Aid*.
I've found the boat we didn't make,
the lake bed's an eyebrow
of the moon. Have you voted.

I've
not

been

myself

since

it

rained

in

my

head

Joke rain
without a punch-line.
Heat ticking in the valley,
a man with 'Boss' on his T-shirt
breast, talking on a mobile phone,
his toddler in a buggy on her own.
I want to shake his arm
gently, say to him,
There is time... is there time
to spellcheck. I'm self-learning
Inuktitut –
the record gets stuck.
What comes after the protocol,
tipping points, ice-core updates
and lunar outposts, the peripheral
visionary's suicide on live TV
sponsored by Gillette.

I've

not

be en

my

self

since

It

r

ained

in

m

y

head

The
things we call providence.
How do you tell the whole story
inside time's labyrinth.
Does it know itself.
What are you saying.
Are you saying.
*Rosie!... Rosie!... She normally
just stays by my side. Thank you*
If this is the last day...
is this the last day.
How 'real' is rain?, Hegel asks,
pulling a brolly from his brain.

I've
     not
been

    my
       self

  since it

rai ned
      in

  my
        he
    ad

I'm through with tenses,
pronouns, lightning
without rain, tension lines
bursting into flames.
You did say... did you
say you have a plan.
I would hide from myself,
if I could, says the sun.

I've

no t

b een

  my
self

sinc

e

it

rain

ed

in

m y

he
ad

What happens to the butterfly
that landed on the rail
where I nearly
place my hand.
Does it enter
here with every start
to look up through
the stanzas towards
and back from
the future to say

I've

not

be en

my

self

since

it

rain ed i

n

m y

hea

d

If you are the rain in my head
I am the Mekong sinking,
particles of sediment
where the current slackened
-off. Silt so plush it barely
registers the second
and third temperature change.
I'm swelling up, running out,
something changes place
with me. 'How many more
wing-nut think tanks,
T-shirt slogans, situations
in the Situation Room?',
the forest and ocean
of the necroscape ask.
I smell the sweet acrid scent
of Sycamore Gap, hear
a bloodshot eye scream
in my head. There is less
and less time that is time.
Have you got the season.

I 've

not

been

myself
          since
it
          rained
     in
my
head

                    I feel so close
                    to the absent
                    rain shape
                    of a woman
                    sitting on a suitcase
                    in a field of stone.
                    Do you remember.
                    I was behind you,
                    the elephant standing on her
                    front feet, back side in the air
                    by a truck wheel. Accordion,
                    sax and keyboard back score.
                    I wish you would talk to me.

          I've
     not
          been

          myself

     since
          it

               r ained

     in

my

head

How it rained for days...
years of having
not wanting to know.
Henri's beach kiosk was a flag,
taking pictures of hailstones,
like golf balls – 86 mph,
'the TV's gone, its 'orrible'.
Where is the enemy.
To whom am I talking.
Am I entering or leaving
pre, post, late fog,
Homo-economicus
and Shona rain-making
in Great Greedington-on
-Disregard. Is it our climate
that is not serious or us.

. I've

not

been

m yself

since

it

r
ained

                    i n

        my

                    head

                    Is there a destination.
                    I feel so close
                    to the woman who
                    throws back her head
            arcing her braids in the glare
                    of a cab, the driver
                    steps out to instant rain,
                    simple thread pulling us
            through. I watch her disappear
                    in a bonfire of hands,
            her spine one wave of saltpetre.

Body – my Yogi, my Horse, my Shadow,

how will I levitate in the exercise yard
without your mantras of tantric Vishnu?
Am I to be found in your pineal gland,
your ventricles? Where is the borderline
between your adenoids and my poetry?

Body, my yogi, my horse, my shadow,

I am your House of Jinn Mirrors
enchanting the air in which you walk.
Who bound us together? If I turn left
and you turn right where Edges meet
what happens to my shoulder's exile?

Body, my yogi, my horse, my shadow,

I know kneecaps have needs, hamstrings
are a racket. I want to hook up
with your brain case and thigh bone
where the branch was sawn off,
gallop towards my father's wrist
and spirit level, my mother's continuum.
You are an animal of tiny silences,
a crow in the sun, the spider and the fly,
the writer and the written.

Body, my yogi, my horse, my shadow,
I like what you can do for me,
marvel at you reading a book
in the sitting position at 40,000 feet. Body,
right now I exist outside you,
a song of the lame contortionist. I can hear
my bones grinding in the other room.

If you mess with my tessitura
I'll shatter your Adam's apple. Body,
if only I'd chosen a different model,
The Bearded Emperor Tamarin, for example.

Body, my yogi, my horse, my shadow,

I leave you my Che Guevara beret
with the red-star third-eye,
I'm doing the inventory.
I have pictures of the wall on my wall,
used paint in the shape of a door. Body,
you are the Rain Antelope's cure
the galloping other life, horses
made of children and grazing.
I enter through your loin at the earth's core,
a stouthearted mustang with planetary eyes
that hurtle across the salt plain like comets.

Body, my yogi, my horse, my shadow,

land smoulders like a cracked brick,
a line of tanks glinting on the bridge.
To whom do I report this?
I was born to dance between tongue
and bone, to the shape of lacking.
Someone inside you is moving your
hand, writing in another nakedness.

Body, my yogi, my horse, my shadow,

you have the innocent magic,
does it matter you play dead,
dissemble the vigilance in me,
give me jaw-cracking glances? Body,
you can't buy me
not even in a dream's auction.
I've discovered a strength,
air sacs and bronchial tubes,
thirty sacs of testosterone gel.
I'll set your plasma on fire.
What's it come to between us?
You taught me so much.

Body, my yogi, my horse, my shadow,

you are the mouth of the source,
a monument to rain, presentiment
to Sanskrit and pearl diving in Bora Bora.
How will I break
on the glinting azure blades
to pace the decks, haunting jelly fish,
lemon tang, Moby Dick, cross-body lead
octopi, without your foam clogged beard
and one live leg, out-echoed
by your ivory peg. May I call you Ahab!
Last time we separated
I took up mindfulness.

Body, my yogi, my horse, my shadow,

are you in front or behind my mirror
of syllables, a deficit of attention
or too much? Body, I've a good mind
to leave the pair of you together,
you and my aorta, you and my yogi, my
horse, my shadow, for my sixth or tenth,
other. She'll wield a rapier baton
return to you with a failed kidney.

Body, my yogi, my horse, my shadow,

your calf strokes this chair leg.
I don't demand fidelity from you.
Someone sows someone, the game goes on.

Where is the border that wanders
between silence and music,
memory and its enunciation?
Body, you shuffle the cards,
finger and thumb vanishing tricks,
secret drops and false transfers.
Can you translate the rain?

Body, my yogi, my horse, my shadow,

I have an unconscious bias
towards being unconscious.
I finish this poem on closing time
and by the morning
you are at my door wanting to talk.

The Searchers

He's John Wayne
siting astride
the armchair arm
waiting for chips and egg
watching Robin Hood
backing up a stone stairway,
long before *Stir Crazy,*
Support Your Local Sheriff.

He's the Lone Ranger,
masked to hide the wrinkles
of that other face, wrinkles
without a face, Tonto
reading smoke signals
speaking non-native. He's
John Wayne, elbows cocked
and poised like springs,
shoulders and hips
toppling into the swagger
along Bedford Road, finger
tap of stetson brim on reachin'
Standard Fireworks, side
stepping Olivia de Havilland
as Lady Marion Fitzwater (who
puts on her tights and fights).
He loves her border-breaking
smile. On the wrong set he's
someone else's tracking shot,
holding a table fork in the first
episode, a blister bubble from
a water bottle on the back
of his hand. He's David Jansen's
Dr Kimble incognito, thankful

for the bread truck's high axle,
time bursting out
of green spiked skin. Caged air

in Religious Education, dreams
of living on *Gilligan's Island*.
The school doctor asking him
to say the first unguarded word
in response to his prompts:

'Fire': 'Fire!'

'Cat': 'Fire!'

'Father': 'Fire!'

'I think that's enough for today.'

'Fire!'

'That was my word, Stephen.'

'Fire!'... 'In the bike shed... Fire!'

Memory is an eye half-closed
working on him day
and night. He is a *where*
and *when* but not a *who*,
putting together pieces
lifted from a sack of shadows,
he's on the wrong side
in someone else's mirage,
cowboy movie posters shot up
in the battle for Hue City.
He's John Wayne, denim turn-ups,
cap-gun holstered, flat feet
– tamping a brittle grizzle of seed

and pinion, a brown, black,
pool of blood on cobblestone paving
outside the Portland Hotel pub,
revolving doors unwinding pneumatic
sighs, cheekbones, cutout eyes,
peering through the ecto-haze
of Players, Park Drive – to find him
cliff-hanging where the end
and beginning are the same
past and future. Every time
he seeks himself he finds a silhouette,
drinking light lifted from the sea
like glass. 'Marina, Aqua Marina,
what are these strange enchantments
that start whenever you're near...'
He is dreamer and dream,
garden and shade, afternoon tea
with Lady Penelope, Bald Eric
creosoting the fence – *Touch this stuff*
'n' yah hair falls out. Virgil Tracy
coming under fire from the US Navy,
Cat Woman running a pet shop,
robbing a crime boss and John Pilger
corresponding from the Mekong Delta
for the Daily Mirror, this,
before Bachman Turner Overdrive
stutters, 'b b b baby you ain't seen
nothing yet', dressed in Yak hair
north west of Moose Jaw and they
give the Nobel Peace Prize to Kissinger.

Crowded out of himself, the Fugitive
of aliases, chasing down the 'One
-armed Man' he sees in his headlights
with the opening credit. He is the silt
vague mirror of rain that returns him
searching for the niece Comanche

rescue – the unmade western he
wants to star in by Cormac McCarthy.

It takes so long for them to say goodbye,
needle jumping in the groove
of 'A Hard Day's Night'
on the saloon jukebox.

'When I'm home everything'
'When I'm home everything'
'When I'm home everything'

Workshop

Thank you for sharing your poem *Anti-love – a resume*, with
    us today.
I love the opening, the directness and power of *Must I refuse/*
or be refused/ and the quoted speech... *it's not on, it's not off/*
it's not even not on or not off. / You remind me of the Crusades.

I think it's the 'standpoint' switches I find confusing from ...
when I move you move, to... *She dropped a screw driver he*
picked it up ... and... *They owned identical shiatzus...*
all in the opening stanza! Maybe I'm missing the point

love exceeds itself to become its opposite but I want to know who
is whom? Is the author/poet the 'I' and who is the beloved? I like
your description of paint, *one tidal wave*, thrown on the
    windscreen
of *an adorable electric convertible* (I own one myself). Again, who
is the vandal: the victim? I do wonder if the metaphysical
    questions

add to your poem? *Is everything that ends, a sequel? /* (Do you mean
prequel?) / *Do we share a now? / When do we share a now?/*
    I love his
jealousy of her relationship with digital Algo. He finds himself
as if with her on Facebook and Skype. Your poem is at its best

when sensuous and visual ... *a water slick arm /*
reaches over the porcelain rim/ for a can of Speckled Hen. I can see
those tiny diamonds of condensation on the ring pull, a collar
    bone
through steam's soft lens. I'm not so sure about 'r' 'u' and 'yr'

('are', 'you' and 'your'). Do these typographic gestures denote
the speeding up of time, the two-dimensional acceleration of love
divided by anti-love under the algorithm's dominatrix or do you
have a faulty keyboard? I am sure about... *For every ennui, there is
an equal and opposite ennui.* Lovely! What a pity you don't do more

with the watering-can metaphor. Sprung-leaks sapping love's grubs,
rusted arguments, blocked spouts of communication... Maybe not!
I love *Purrit int Bin*. Ditto: *The sun-rinsed breakfast room, smell
of toasting bread – 'pop' they're done!* I feel it could end here
but no, there's more, maybe your point. If this end is an end

it doesn't end with us. There is a memorable poem in this poem,
maybe two or even three. Please, more on the *Mirage's light*
and *the Hummingbird's ink*, presumably alluding to the 'how' we
choose to write about love? As for your style – serenade,
    experience,
deviate. Don't track the traces, be the horse that falls from the poem
into itself. Ask – is this all of me? Ignore all advice.

PS

Hare Krishna Hare Krishna
Krishna Krishna Hare Hare
Hare Rama Hare Rama
Rama Rama Hare Hare

What a tenuous link, my lost *Hare Krishna Chant and be
    Happy* bookmark!
To sleep awake in the skin of words of trusted theft
    and gift, my ear, this book.

'What's it about?' my friend asks and since no-thing is
    ever just blind spots or shadows,
want to say, *Owl did that bird of prey get in my frothy cup ...
read my book!*

Krishna Krishna Hare Hare. I know: no 'I'. How strange,
    this freedom in chains
of signs passing through coming out the other side of time
    as image, book.

Between samsara and nirvana, pencil in my hand
    as if sense
is an echo of sound – *Do you have a song request towards
a coffee luv* – a different page in the same book,

written by the 'I' in the 'We' in the 'I'. I know who I am!
    Parallel dreams fit inside this book.
I say to the earth: Is it too late? A tree grows in gutter rain.
    Call for the Hare Krishna CookBook!

What a tenuous link, the Sunday Love Feast! *Krishna Hare*
     this pathless
path of the always dissolving border crossing, a place we
     share this mind, book.

Words not outsmarting but outfacing like 'The Guv'nors'
     standing in the ruins wearing Sunday suits
in Don McCullin's rite of passage photograph, one image
     can save a life. One book?

Hare Rama Hare Rama. I follow these words in the search.
     What a tenuous link,
my lost *Hare Krishna Chant and be Happy* bookmark!
     I receive my 'no-self' 'self'
from a river's hidden camera, the watery pages of this book.

If stanzas are 'rooms,' I need a loft extension. Laughter is
     burning Krishna's chemise.
If I don't make it happen: the woman grabbing the goose
     that grabs her book.

If I don't make it happen, a long-in-the-face thoroughbred
     nuzzling my fingertips, her ear
keen as a dog's nose. I love that Krishna slow, quick, chant
     inside this book.

When words are not enough
     Jenny Erpenbeck takes up the slanted pen...
'Not a Novel.' What then? From silence to silence,
     a teaspoon of light, the translatable book.

Acknowledgements

'Through the Wall' was first published in *The Living and the Dead: Creative Conversations between Past and Present* (2019). 'Notes on Time' was published in *RE-IMAGINING AGEING: An Exhibition of Poetry* (2021).

I am grateful to Debjani Chatterjee, Eleonora Bonzagni, Angelina D'Roza, Jennifer Donnison, Louise Dore, Chris Jones, Janet Murray, Julia Podziewska, Karl Riordan, Phillip Sawyer, Stephen Spencer and Helen Williams for their various and generous responses during the writing of this collection. I would like to acknowledge all the writers of the Sheffield Central Library's Creative Writing and Poetry Workshops, past and present, for your friendly insight and encouragement.

To Claire Walker – a special thank you for your advice, support and patience over the long haul.

Notes

Makes it Rain
Written after the death of a rough sleeper in Sheffield in 2020 and the swift removal by Sheffield City Council of the impromptu memorial of flowers, cards and lighted candles in the Arundel Gate subway, Sheffield city centre. Winston Wolf is a character played by Harvey Keitel in Quentin Tarantino's *Pulp Fiction* (1994). The Wolf's speciality is disposing of evidence left behind by Marsellus Wallace's crime cartel based in Los Angeles, California.

Narcissus' Graves Park Song
The Happiest Days of Your Life is a 1950 British comedy film directed by Phillip Launder, starring Margaret Rutherford and Alastair Sim.

Ode to the Paint Brush
Robert Tressell (1870–1911) wrote *The Ragged Trousered Philanthropists*. He spent his early working life in South Africa. DIY SOS was a BBC DIY television series (1999–2010). 'Hands that do dishes are as soft as your face' is a line from a song in a TV advert for a brand of washing up liquid. *Double Your Money* was a popular British TV quiz show (1955–1964) hosted by Hughie Green. Martin Luther King was assassinated at the Lorraine Motel in Memphis Tennessee in 1968. Thunderbird Five was International Rescue's space station responsible for relaying distress calls from around the world.

1.5 Metres of Earth
PPE refers to Personal protective equipment. In Greek mythology Atlas is condemned by Zeus to hold up the sky for eternity as a punishment for joining the Titans in their war against the Olympus. The French novelist Albert Camus (1913–60) was an admirer of Herman Melville's novel *Moby Dick* (1851). Jürgen

Klopp is a football manager (Borussia Dortmund and Liver-pool) associated with the high intensity counter-pressing style of play high up the pitch called *gengenpressing*. In 1649, a group of 'Diggers' established an agricultural commune at St George's Hill, near Weybridge in Surrey. Leon Rosselson's song *The World Turned Upside Down* commemorates the Digger movement.

Notes on Time
Inuit Nunangat translates as 'the place where Inuit live'.

Season of Unlocking
'When I'm out on a quiet spree' is from Cole Porter's *I Get a Kick Out Of You*. The naked child running on a road is nine-year-old Phan Thi Kim Phúc, burned by the napalm bombing of Trang Bang by the US in 1972. Isabel Archer is the title character of Henry James' *Portrait of a Lady* (1881). Raskolnikov and Sonia are the two main characters in Dostoevsky's *Crime and Punishment* by Fyodor (1866). Jay Gatsby is a major character in F Scott Fitzgerald's *The Great Gatsby* (1925). The phrase, 'I look like Cousin Itt!', refers to the fictional character in *The Addams Family* TV series (1964), whose visible form is composed almost entirely of floor length hair. During the Covid pandemic people could not access a hair stylist or barbershop because of govern-ment Coronavirus lockdowns and restrictions.

Knitting Witch was written in the tailspin of media interest in Captain Sir Tom Moore (1920–2021).

Contagion
In *Blindness,* a novel by Portuguese author José Saramago, a city is struck by a plague of White Blindness.

All That's Solid Melts into Air
'Fearless Girl' is a bronze sculpture by Kristen Visbal, commis-sioned by State Street Global, a New York asset-management company. It was first installed, near the Charging Bull statue on Wall Street in 2017.

Sabrina
Onegin and Tatyana are characters in Alexander Pushkin's *Eugene Onegin* (1825). 'I can't see ya, but I know you're here. I can feel it,' is said by Peter Falk in Wim Wenders' 1987 film *Wings of Desire*. 'That's Life' is a popular song written by Dean Kay and Kelly Gordon and first recorded in 1963 by Marion Montgomery.

The Great Plains
Layli Long Soldier is an Oglala Lakota poet, writer, feminist and activist. The Oglala Lakota are one of the many tribes of the Sioux Nation whose ancestral homeland are the Great Plains of western South Dakota and Wyoming.

Ode to a Donkey Jacket
The Battle of Orgreave took place on 18 June 1984 when police officers from numerous forces ensnared and violently attacked miners picketing outside the British Steel coking plant in Rotherham, South Yorkshire. An independent Police Complaints commission (IPCC) in 2015, found there was 'excessive violence by police officers, a false narrative from police exaggerating violence by miners, perjury by officers giving evidence to prosecute the arrested men, and an apparent cover-up of that perjury by senior officers.'

Tubar Mirabilis
Tubar Mirabilis is a powerful organ reed stop that requires very high wind pressure. Also called Tubar Major. The Grand Organ in the Albert Hall was originally described as the Voice of Jupiter by its builder Henry Willis. Originally built in 1871, when it was the largest in the world. *Einstein on the Beach* is an opera in four acts composed by Phillip Glass and directed by Robert Wilson. *4´33˝* is a composition by the American experimental composer John Cage. *Six Pianos* is a minimalist piece by the American experimental composer Steve Reich. He also composed a variation for six marimbas, called Six Marimbas, in 1986.

Ghosted

Marlene Dietrich's Beaded Illusional Gown is displayed (or exhibited) at the Filmmuseum Düsseldorf. *Eyes Wide Shut* (1999) was directed by Stanley Kubrick. *You Want It Darker* was Leonard Cohen's last studio album.

Body – my Yogi, my Horse, my Shadow

The term tessitura refers to the most comfortable vocal range for a singer or musical instrument. Captain Ahab is a fictional character and one of the protagonists in Herman Melville's 1851 novel *Moby Dick*.

The Searchers

The Searchers is a 1956 film directed by John Ford and starring John Wayne as a civil war veteran. *Aqua Marina*, was the ending theme of Gerry and Sylvia Anderson's 1960s TV series *Stingray*. *The Fugitive* was a long-running 1960s TV series created by Roy Huggins and starring David Janssen as Dr Kimble, who is wrongfully convicted of his wife's murder. The Battle for Hue City was the scene of the longest and bloodiest battle of the 1968 Tet Offensive during which North Vietnamese and Vietcong forces engaged the South Vietnamese and U.S forces. In 1973 Henry Kissinger was awarded the Nobel Peace Prize.

PS

Written in response to a creative writing workshop exercise that involved a variety of stimuli including a 'Hare Krishna Chant and be Happy' bookmark. *Guvnors, Finsbury Park Gang, 1958* is a famous photograph taken by the British photojournalist Don McCullin. Jenny Erpenbeck is a German writer and opera director.